Kenny
Wild's Hair

KENNY WILD'S hAiR

by Janet Greeson
illustrations by
Leigh Grant

FRANKLIN WATTS / 1989
NEW YORK / LONDON
TORONTO / SYDNEY

Special thanks to Jerry Rogers, Sandra Posey,
Cheryl Lyall, and all the wild, wonderful
Westwood Wolverines I've taught during the
last nine years.

Library of Congress Cataloging-in-Publication Data
Greeson, Janet, 1952–
Kenny Wild's hair / by Janet Greeson;
illustrations by Leigh Grant.
p. cm.
Summary: Tired of being nagged by his parents
about his messy hair, ten-year-old Kenny Wild
makes a wish for really wild hair—a wish he
soon comes to regret.
ISBN 0-531-15118-2. — ISBN 0-531-10792-2 (lib. bdg.)
[1. Hair—Fiction.   2. Schools—Fiction.   3.
Humorous stories.]
I. Grant, Leigh, ill.   II. Title.
PZ7.G8536Ke   1989
[Fic]—dc19   89-31167   CIP   AC

Contents

for Jim

Chapter
One / Sawdust
for Breakfast

"Breakfast never tastes like breakfast when you're in trouble," Kenny said. He pushed his nearly full bowl of Wheaties toward the middle of the kitchen table and sighed.

"I know what you mean, little brother," Valerie agreed, nodding her head wisely. "Your cereal must taste like sawdust. Even I, the poor unfortunate forced to live with you for ten long years and witness the incredibly stupid stunts you come up with, can't believe what you did last night. What could you have been thinking?"

She smiled at the end of her little speech, a big-sister smile. The goody-goody smile the best behaved child of the family uses on the one in trouble. Sometimes Kenny got to use the goody-goody smile, but not nearly as often as Valerie. She was five years older than Kenny and much better at staying out of trouble.

"I'm the unfortunate one. I'm the one in trouble." Kenny's voice grew louder and louder. "And I know exactly what I was thinking. I was trying to be helpful! Dad didn't understand!"

"I know. How could a face get so red? That was bad, but not as bad as when he came back from the garage. I've never seen Dad cry before," Valerie said. She stared at her left leg and foot. Today she wore only two socks on each foot.

"He never cried! He almost cried, but he didn't really. It wasn't that bad," Kenny said.

Bending over, Valerie carefully scrunched her orange sock down on top of her left shoe, exposing more of the pink sock she wore under the orange one. She pulled the pink sock up over her left pant leg.

"That's a matter of opinion. In my opinion, and Dad's, it's the worst thing you've ever done. I know you were only trying to be helpful. But you should have learned by now that trying to be helpful always gets you in trouble. You've really got to give up those stupid Helpfulness Plots. They never work. If you would just comb your hair and look like a normal person, you wouldn't need your stupid old HPs."

Left side adjusted to her satisfaction, Valerie turned her attention to her right leg and

foot. On that side, she wore green and purple socks. She scrunched the purple sock down to expose the green sock underneath it. Finally, she pulled the green sock up over her right pant leg. Her shoes were silver, her ankle-zipped jeans black. Her cotton sweater, which hung below her knees, contained all the colors available in a box of twenty-four Crayola crayons.

Five ribbons, one yellow, one red, one orange, one green and a multicolor striped one, all knotted together, perched on the right side of her hair. Their ends, each a different length, streamed down her right shoulder. It was Monday morning, and Valerie was ready for a day at Elmwood High.

She picked up her books and jacket. Buttons, badges and patches covered her jacket's blue denim sleeves. The buttons said things like, WHO, ME?, IN YOUR FACE, STEP ON IT and AREN'T YOU LUCKY.

"You should be comforting me, not rubbing it in."

"Kenny, what you did was so bad my comfort won't help."

"Don't leave me, Val, please. Stay with me while Dad 'deals' with me. Do me this one favor and I'll do anything you ask."

"Anything? Even give me your Screaming Skulls ticket?"

The Screaming Skulls were Valerie and Kenny's favorite rock group. Next month, the Skulls were giving a concert in Valerie and Kenny's hometown. Kenny was radio station KWAZ's tenth lucky listener to call in and scream, "I rock with KWAZ!" His prize was a ticket to the Skulls' concert. The Skulls ticket was Kenny's most valued possession.

"Anything but that."

"That's what I thought. If I didn't have such a weak stomach, I'd stick around anyway." She started out the door, paused and said, "Wearing Aunt Adeline's birthday present won't help. See ya later, creep, if you're still alive."

When the door slammed, Kenny's whole body sagged. He slid down in his chair, limp all over, like last night's pasta. Even his hair didn't stick out, well, not as much as usual. Kenny Wild's hair matched his name. He liked his wild hair, his family didn't. Valerie claimed he styled his hair by kissing an air conditioner that was turned on high. Actually, Kenny didn't style his hair. He didn't even comb it.

Chapter
Two / The
Perfect Car

Valerie went to school, leaving Kenny alone in his misery. He leaned forward, placed his elbows on the table, closed his eyes and sighed again.

He remembered every detail of the terrible event clearly, as if it had happened yesterday. Actually, it did happen yesterday, a quiet Sunday. Sunday night to be exact.

After last night's dinner (Kenny's favorite, spaghetti and meatballs) he boogied upstairs to his room and started his math homework, multiplying decimals. After working ten problems, he boogied back downstairs to get a Coke.

At the kitchen door, Kenny paused and listened. Well, some people might call it eavesdropping, since his parents had no idea he was there. The Wilds rotated turns for kitchen chores, parents one night, children the next. Kenny's mom and dad discussed their workday's events on their chore nights. He over-heard some pretty interesting stuff on those nights.

Sometimes, Kenny and Valerie did the same thing on their chore nights, then their parents overheard some pretty interesting stuff. Kenny and Valerie never imagined their parents would eavesdrop. Kenny didn't feel guilty about eavesdropping. He always used the information he overheard for one of his Helpfulness Plots, or HPs as he called them. HPs required good planning. Good planning required lots of information. Eavesdropping was the best way to get it. Kenny planned his HPs with the best of intentions. They were supposed to help his family.

Kenny's dad was talking. "It's beautiful, Beth, drives like a dream. I've always wanted one and I got such a deal on it." As he loaded the dishwasher, Jim Wild, Kenny's father, smiled at the thought of his good deal.

Kenny stayed hidden outside the door. *Oh no*, he thought. *Dad must have bought another car.* Mr. Wild was quite a wheeler dealer when it came to cars. The Wild family had owned twenty-seven cars in the last five years.

"Hand me the leftover spaghetti and I'll put it away," Kenny's mother, Beth Wild, said. "I'm glad you finally found THE car you've always wanted, because I want to keep this one. No more cars for a while. I've had enough."

"Well, it's just what I've always wanted, except for one little thing," Mr. Wild said as he passed the spaghetti.

"Oh no, you don't. We're keeping it anyway. Really, Jim, I was so embarrassed the day I finished shopping, couldn't find the car and called the police to report it stolen. After three hours they found it in the mall parking lot. It had been there the whole time. And they weren't very nice either. They didn't understand that a person can forget what her car looks like when she's had six cars in the last year." Mrs. Wild put the leftover spaghetti in a Tupperware bowl and put the bowl in the refrigerator.

"I know, Beth, I know," Mr. Wild said soothingly.

"And then there're all the times I've been late because I can't remember how to unlock the steering wheel on a new car or tried to use an old car key on a new car. Do you know how many locksmiths I've called and how expensive they are?" she demanded and waited for his answer.

"I keep telling you, throw the old car keys away. Then you won't have that problem."

She ignored his answer. "We've just got to keep this car. We're not trading it off. I insist."

She hesitated, "What kind of car is it, anyway?"

"It's a new Corvette Stingray, candy-apple red."

Mrs. Wild's eyes glazed over at the thought of taking Kenny to soccer games, the dog to the vet, Valerie to gymnastics and doing the grocery shopping in a sports car with two seats. "A sports car! Twenty-seven cars in five years and I've always managed to talk you out of a sports car. Oh, all right, I give up. I still want to keep it."

"Great. I'm glad you want the car. It's sitting in our garage." Mr. Wild said and grinned. "I didn't want to tell the kids until we'd discussed it. Come on." He opened the door to the garage and motioned his wife through. "Let's go look at it. We'll tell the kids tomorrow."

"What is the one little thing that keeps it from being exactly what you've always wanted?" Mrs. Wild asked as she walked into the garage.

"No pinstripes. But that's easily taken care of. One day I'll have pinstripes put down both sides," Mr. Wild said, following his wife into the garage. "Don't worry, Beth, I'm working on a deal for a station wagon. I got such a great deal on the 'Vette, we can afford two cars."

No pinstripes. Great, Kenny thought. *This'll make a super HP.* By the time his parents came back into the house, Kenny was nowhere near the kitchen. He was in his room, planning the pinstripe HP. He should have stayed there.

Chapter
Three / The
Pinstripe Fiasco

"If only I could go back in time," Kenny moaned. "Just to last night and undo what happened. Last night, if someone had told me I was planning the great pinstripe fiasco, I wouldn't have believed them."

It seemed like hours after Valerie left for school. Actually it was two minutes. Kenny walked over to the telephone and dialed the number of Pete Williams, his best friend. The phone only rang once before Kenny heard a click and a voice say, "Pete's Pizza. We deliver."

Kenny knew it was Pete. He and Pete had been best friends since kindergarten. Back then they liked to phone each other and talk animal. Cow was Kenny's favorite. Pete preferred gorilla.

"Hi, Pete."

"Hi, Kenny. What's up? Wanna come over and walk to school with me?"

"No, I'm in big trouble again. I can't go anywhere until Dad talks to me and he's not up yet."

"What happened?"

"Well, you know how Dad always nags me about not using my 'Design Your Own Sports Car' kit, the one he gave me last Christmas." Before Kenny could say more, he heard another click.

"Lo! Lo! Sammy talk too," a voice screamed into the telephone. Kenny held the receiver as far away from his ear as he could reach. He still heard the voice clearly.

"Get off!" Pete yelled. "This is for me, not you. Get off, you little jerk."

"Sammy good. Sammy talk good. Sammy sing good."

The voice stopped. Kenny heard heavy breathing, then the voice bellowed, "Sing! Sing song! Sing! Sing a song."

"I'm going to get you, you little brat." Pete snarled. Kenny heard Pete's receiver hit the floor and Pete's footsteps, running for Sammy. Sammy was Pete's two-year-old little pest, sometimes known as a little brother. Next, Kenny heard screams and a door slam. Then Pete was back. "What a monster. Where were we? Oh yeah, your kit. Your dad does say the kit cost too much to be used so little. So you used it, right?"

"Right, I wanted to surprise Dad," Kenny said quickly. Sammy might pick up the phone again any minute. "See, Dad got a new car, but he wanted pinstripes on the sides and it didn't have any. Well, last night, I used the Magic Markers from my 'Design Your Own Sports Car' kit to draw pinstripes along both sides of the car. He wasn't at all pleased after I called him to come look, and he came, and he looked."

"Slow down. I locked Sammy in the hall closet. He won't bother us again. So what's your dad gonna do to you?"

"I don't know. He was very upset. The fact that I used a purple Magic Marker seemed to upset him even more. When he was able to talk again, he said pinstripes should be painted on with paint, not drawn on with Magic Marker, and they should be black, not purple. I'd just offered to paint over the Magic Marker, when he lost his voice, again."

"Wow! If he was that mad, whatever he does, it's gonna be awful."

"I know. After my offer, I could tell he was counting to ten, silently, like Mom used to make me do when I was real little and dumb and about to throw a tantrum."

"You mean last year," Pete interrupted.

"Ha, ha, very funny. Anyway, that seemed to help. He was able to talk again and he said he would deal with me this morning and sent me to my room. He hasn't come downstairs yet."

"Let me guess, the pinstripes were another one of your HPs, right?"

"Right."

"You should stop using those. You know they always get you in trouble."

"I know. I've finally figured that out." Kenny heard the stairs creak. "I gotta go, Pete, I think my parents are up."

"Okay, call me later"—he paused—"if you're still alive. Bye."

"Bye, Pete." Kenny hung up the phone. The stairs creaked again. His parents must be awake and on their way to the kitchen, to deal with him.

Chapter
Four / Grounded

Kenny thought about running away before his parents made it to the kitchen, but he was wearing Aunt Adeline's birthday present. He only wore it when he was in trouble, just to please his mother, Aunt Adeline's sister. Wearing it seemed like a good idea last night, but this morning he realized his mistake. He would never be seen in public wearing pink Care Bear pajamas, with feet. He would have to run away naked.

Running away naked was out. Kenny felt his forehead with the back of one hand. It felt warm. Maybe he was sick. If he was sick his dad wouldn't punish him. He started for the downstairs bathroom to take his temperature.

The stairs creaked again. He stopped. Maybe it wasn't his parents. Maybe it was an ax murderer, like in the movie he saw last week, "Friday the 13th, part 27." Instead of his parents coming down the creaky stairs, maybe a crazed slobbering ax killer was sneaking up the creaky stairs, on his way to the bedroom where Kenny's unsuspecting parents lay sleeping.

If Kenny could save them, his dad would forgive him for the pinstripes. He would be a hero. He would get his name in the newspaper, maybe his photograph too. *Perfect*, Kenny thought. *Here's a mini HP made to order to get me out of trouble for the pinstripe fiasco.*

A weapon. He needed a weapon. He looked frantically around the kitchen for something to use as a weapon. "Box of cereal, bowl of cereal, cereal spoon," he mumbled as he searched. "Nope, nope, no good. There must be something I can use. Enduro Superstick, olive oil, pickles, plastic wrap." He paused when he saw the wooden knife rack sitting on the counter. "No knives, no knives. I don't like blood," he mumbled, and kept searching.

The stairs creaked again. Kenny knew every creak took the crazed ax murderer closer to his innocent parents. He couldn't waste any more time looking for a weapon. "I knew I should have taken karate lessons," he said and grabbed something off the counter. It was the tube of Enduro Superstick. "Maybe I can sneak up behind him and glue his feet to the floor. Hope it works better on feet than it does on glass," Kenny muttered.

He rushed out the kitchen door. He didn't get far. Just outside the door, he ran into his dad. Kenny fell on top of Mr. Wild and Mr. Wild fell on top of Mrs. Wild. For a few moments, they all lay in a pile on the floor, too stunned to move. Mr. Wild was the first to react. "Get off us, Kenny!" he shouted and shoved Kenny onto the floor.

"I think you hurt me, Dad." Kenny moaned and rolled around on the floor. "Great, he thought, *this is better than running a temperature*. Oh, my arm. I can't move my arm. I think it's broken."

"Get up, Kenny. You fell on us. We're the ones who might be hurt." Mr. Wild stood up. "Well, I'm all right. How about you, dear?" He took hold of his wife's hands and pulled her to her feet. "Any bones broken?"

"I'm fine, thanks." Mrs. Wild stood, looked down at Kenny and said, "Kenny, you can stop faking. Your dad's calmed down. The car is okay. After hours of rubbing, I got your pinstripes to come off the car."

Kenny stopped moaning and rolling. He looked up at his mother and asked, "Really? Thanks, Mom!" He jumped up, turned to his father and said, "Dad, I'm sorry about the pinstripes. I was only trying to be helpful, honest."

"I know, Kenny, I know. Just give up your Helpfulness Plots. Don't use them on us anymore, okay?"

"Okay, Dad."

"By the way, you're grounded for a month." Mr. Wild started to walk into the kitchen, paused and said, "And no allowance while you're grounded. Now take those silly pajamas off and get dressed for school." He walked into the kitchen.

"Bye, honey," Mrs. Wild said. "I like your pajamas." She smiled at Kenny. "Hurry or you'll be late." She followed her husband into the kitchen.

"Bye, Mom," Kenny said.

He went to his room, dressed quickly and left for his school, Westdale Elementary. It was a cloudy, chilly February day. A day that matched Kenny's mood. "Being grounded for a month, four whole weeks, is worse than being dead," he muttered. As Kenny walked to school, he thought about his HPs.

Chapter
Five / Helpfulness Plots

Kenny's hair forced him to use HPs. Well, it wasn't actually his hair, it was that he didn't comb his hair. All his life he'd hated to comb his hair. About a year ago, he cut back on his hair combing. For a while he combed it once a day, then once a week, then only once a month.

Several weeks ago, after his last haircut, he stopped combing it at all. Now his hair stuck out all over. On a scale of one to ten, ten being the wildest, Kenny's hair would be a twenty-five. Kenny insisted his hair was only slightly messy, not wild. He thought he looked like David Dude, lead singer of the Skulls.

Kenny didn't mind washing his hair. His wild hair was very clean. In fact, he washed his hair every night with Manly Guy Shampoo, to give it body—just like the Manly Guy commercial said, "If you've got no body, get some body. Use Manly Guy Shampoo." Kenny's hair had a lot of body, especially when he went to bed with it wet. Then it really stuck out the next morning.

At first, his family ignored his hair. They hoped Kenny would "come to his senses" and start combing his hair again. He didn't. One by one they tried to get him to comb his hair.

Valerie tried shaming him. She said, "Kenny, comb your hair. You don't look like David Dude. You look stupid. Everyone combs their hair. Besides, your hair embarrasses me. I don't want my friends to know you're my brother. I don't even want them to see you."

"I don't want your friends to see me either." Kenny stuck his tongue out at his sister.

"Forget it, Kenny. I wouldn't want my friends to know you're my brother, even if you did comb your hair."

Mr. Wild tried bribery. "Kenny," he said, "if you comb your hair I'll give you five dollars." He waved a five-dollar bill in Kenny's face.

"How about five thousand dollars, Dad? I think I could do it for five thousand."

"Never mind, Kenny. For five thousand dollars I'll stop combing my hair." Mr. Wild frowned. "Sometimes I wish I believed in corporal punishment."

Kenny's mother tried reasoning with him and making him feel guilty. "Kenny," she said gently, "please comb your hair. You know it upsets your father and me for you to go around looking so, so unkempt. It's such a small thing to ask, but it would mean a lot to us." She smiled sweetly at him and patted his hand.

"I'm sorry, Mom, really I am. I want to be good, but I hate to comb my hair. I just can't do it." He reached over, patted her hand and smiled. "Don't make such a big deal out of it. At least I don't spray my hair purple like some of Valerie's friends."

When shame, bribery, reason and guilt failed, Kenny knew their next tactic would be brute force. Maybe tying him to a chair and shaving his head, or combing his hair for him. He thought a long time about the brute-force problem. Finally, he had the perfect answer. Helpfulness Plots, or HPs.

His HPs would be super helpful to his family, so super helpful, they would make his family forget all about hair and brute force. All his parents would notice was what a fine, helpful person they had for a son. And Valerie would think he was the best brother in the world. Yep, after a couple of HPs, Kenny figured he could just relax and never worry about combing his hair again.

His first mistake was telling his family about his HPs. Actually, his first mistake was thinking of HPs. His second mistake was telling his family. His third mistake, the biggest of all, was using HPs. HPs seemed like a great idea, but they didn't always work out as planned. The pinstripe HP wasn't his only failure. Kenny could remember others, several others.

Chapter
Six / HPs Gone Bad

There had been his entertainment HP, the one planned to help Valerie. She ruined that one because she had no sense of humor. For that HP, Kenny entertained Bob Stevens, while Bob waited for Valerie to get ready for their first date. Kenny was sure the time he spent with Bob would be the most fun Bob had all evening.

"Look at this one, Bob."

Bob looked. His face turned bright red. "Uh, yeah. That's nice," Bob said. He sat on the sofa next to Kenny and squirmed.

"How about this one?"

Bob's face and neck turned bright red. "That's nice too, Kenny. Is Valerie almost ready?"

"I don't know. Who cares." Kenny turned another page in the family photograph album. He elbowed Bob in the ribs. "She sure looks weird in this one, doesn't she?"

"Ready, Bob?" Valerie asked as she walked into the room. Kenny closed the album and shoved it under a sofa cushion while Bob stood and walked over to Valerie.

"I sure am. Let's go."

When Valerie got home from her date, she went into Kenny's room and really yelled at him. "Kenny, never ever, on pain of death, unless you want to be staked to an ant hill. Unless you want to spend the rest of your life with a seeing-eye dog. Never entertain. No, never talk. No, never even be in the same room with any date of mine again." She ran out of his room, yelling, "Mother, Mother! Do you know what Kenny did? I'm burning those photos, Mother. He'll never show my potty training pictures to anyone again."

Then there was the wine glass HP, the one planned to help his mother. That HP was ruined by carelessness. Mrs. Wild owned twelve crystal wine glasses. They had been in the family since the beginning of time and were used only for special occasions. Mrs. Wild always washed her glasses once a month, even if they didn't need it.

The wine glass HP was simple. Kenny would wash the glasses. That HP worked nicely for the first nine glasses. The trouble started with the last three, when their stems broke off. Actually, a Nerf football broke the

stems off. Kenny and Pete were just playing indoors catch. Pete was over helping Kenny wash the glasses, but after washing nine glasses, they needed a break.

One quick pass of the old Nerf football seemed like a good idea. Kenny passed the ball, but Pete didn't complete the pass. The last three glasses were sitting on the coffee table, waiting to be carried into the kitchen, when the ball crashed into them.

Kenny decided to glue the stems back on. "Why tell Mom, Pete? It'll only upset her. Look, we'll use Enduro Superstick. Don't worry. It's guaranteed to bond anything forever. No one will ever know."

The Enduro Superstick worked, but not forever. Just until his parents' next special occasion, a dinner party. After their guests left, the Wilds began to clean up. On dinner-party nights the whole family helped with kitchen chores.

Kenny, Valerie, and Mr. Wild sat at the kitchen table, helping by eating leftover party food.

Mrs. Wild stood at the sink, lovingly washing her crystal wine glasses.

"Look at this!" she exclaimed. Mrs. Wild turned from the sink toward her family. She held a glass stem in one hand and the rest of the glass in the other hand.

Kenny's mouth went dry. He no longer wanted the miniature eggroll he had just popped into his mouth. He forced himself to chew and swallow. The eggroll didn't go down all the way.

"The stems on three of them just broke off." Mrs. Wild shook her head. "What a shame. I guess they're more delicate than I thought."

His mom didn't suspect anything. Kenny felt guilty, but he didn't confess. Maybe, when his mom was old and grayer and he was a rich brain surgeon, maybe then he would tell his mom about breaking the glasses. Or maybe not.

Another failure was his tag sale HP, the one planned to help the whole family. For that HP, Kenny made signs for the family's annual tag sale. That HP was ruined by poor planning. He should never have chosen the living room as the place to make the signs.

He spilled six cans of tempera paint powder on the living-room floor. It could have been worse. At least the floor was wood, not carpet. The floor looked like the victim of a tempera paint bomb explosion, until he tried to clean it up with a wet mop instead of the vacuum cleaner. His mom was furious.

"You know, Mom," Kenny said, trying to calm her down, "some mothers would call it art and photograph the floor as a memento of their son's talent. Some mothers, good mothers, would see the humor in this situation and laugh."

"Kenny, you will stay in this room until every drop, every particle of that paint is cleaned up. I don't care if it takes you forty years and you have to lick it up with your tongue." After that HP, Kenny decided Val AND his mom had no sense of humor.

"And my pinstripe HP sure failed," Kenny said to himself as he walked into the school building.

Kenny didn't get into any trouble at school. As he walked home at the end of the day, he felt pretty good. That's because he had no idea what was in store for him when his dad got home. All too soon, Kenny would discover his pinstripe HP not only failed, it backfired.

Chapter
Seven / Hairphobia

When Mr. Wild got home, Kenny was upstairs in his room, lying low. "Kenny, get down here right now," Mr. Wild yelled. "I want to talk to you."

Oh, oh, Kenny thought, walking down the stairs. *He's had a bad day, a very bad day.* Once downstairs, he stood in front of his father and waited.

"Kenny, HPs are a poor excuse for not combing your hair. I'm glad you promised to stop using them on us."

"But, Dad," Kenny interrupted.

"No arguing, just listen. Your mother and I don't believe in forcing you to do something you really don't want to do, but you've forced us into a corner. You've left us no choice."

"But, Dad!"

"No buts, just let me finish. We're not going to make you comb your hair. However, since hair combing is so repulsive to you, your mother and I insist you see Dr. Shoemaker, the school counselor. It's all set. You have an appointment for ten o'clock next Monday morning. Don't miss it."

"Okay, okay, I'll go," Kenny agreed. *Boy,* he thought, *Dad must still be upset about the pin-stripe HP. I've never visited the counselor. I hope she doesn't say there's something awful wrong with me, like hairphobia.* At the beginning of the school year, Kenny's class studied phobias. He knew a phobia was something you were afraid of, like water, that was called hydrophobia. A fear of heights was called acrophobia. *What if there's such a thing as hairphobia and I have it? I don't want hairphobia. It would be terrible to be afraid of your own hair.*

All too soon it was Monday, Dr. Shoemaker Monday. That morning, Kenny walked into his classroom and headed straight for Nicholas Webster's desk. Nicholas visited Dr. Shoemaker a lot. He saw her because when anyone sang "Jolly Old Saint Nicholas" to him, which was pretty often since they knew it bugged him, he cried.

"Hi, Nick," Kenny said. "What's Dr. Shoemaker like? I mean, what happens when you go see her?"

"I cry a lot. She has three boxes of tissues in her office and she doesn't care how many I use. She's very nice. Why?"

"I just wondered. I thought if she gave out candy or something good, I'd go see her, but not for tissues, yuck." Kenny wasn't telling anyone, except Mrs. Welty, his teacher, that he was visiting the counselor. At 9:55, Kenny left his fifth-grade classroom and began the long walk to the counselor's office.

He walked like Bigfoot, slapping each foot flat against the floor, making a loud, floppy noise, guaranteed to drive teachers crazy. Whenever they had a substitute, his whole class Bigfoot-walked everywhere.

At 9:59 he stood outside Dr. Shoemaker's office. He knew it was her office. The sign on the door said, Dr. Shoemaker—School Counselor. He noticed a used tissue on the floor. "I'm scared, but I'm not going to cry. I'm not going to cry," he said over and over to himself, as he knocked on the door.

"Come in, come in," a cheerful voice called.

Kenny opened the door and walked into a small room that wasn't anything like his regular classroom. A bright blue carpet covered the floor. One wall was painted with storybook characters. The other three walls were covered with posters that said things like, "When life gives you lemons, make lemonade," "Have a nice day" and "Bloom where you are planted."

There wasn't much furniture in the room, just a wooden table, a desk, and a few chairs. In the middle of the table was a doll house, a doll family, and a box of Kleenex tissues. Two chairs were placed opposite each other at the table. Bean bag chairs, in bright colors, were piled in one corner, next to a box of Kleenex tissues. A woman sat behind the desk. On the desk was a telephone, a big calendar, a round blue-green stone, and a box of Kleenex tissues. In front of the desk, opposite the woman, was a chair.

"Hello, you must be Kenny Wild," the woman said, standing up and reaching over her desk to shake hands with Kenny. She wore tennis shoes and blue jeans and she was smiling. "I'm Dr. Shoemaker. Please sit down." She pointed to the chair in front of her desk. Kenny sat. "Now, Kenny," she said kindly. "Most people come to see me because they have something they need to talk about, do you? Will you tell me why you're here?"

"My parents made me come," Kenny said.

"I see," Dr. Shoemaker said.

Kenny waited. So did Dr. Shoemaker. She was better at waiting than Kenny. He broke down and said, "My parents made me come because I hate to comb my hair. Actually, I won't comb it."

"I see," Dr. Shoemaker said.

After a few minutes Kenny said, "They say my hair is wild. I don't think it's wild. It's just slightly messy."

"I see," Dr. Shoemaker said. Kenny decided counselors must be trained at a very early age not to be surprised at anything and to say "I see" all the time. "Kenny," she continued, "have you ever heard a light-bulb joke?"

"Yeah, lots of them. I even made one up. Well, not exactly the whole thing. I just changed one a little. It's my favorite. Do you want to hear it?"

"Yes, Kenny, please tell it."

"How many big sisters does it take to change a light bulb?"

"I don't know, Kenny. How many?"

"It takes five. Four to turn the ladder and one to hold the light bulb." Kenny laughed a long time. He could never tell that joke without cracking up.

Dr. Shoemaker smiled and said, "That's a good one, Kenny. There's a counselor's light-bulb joke, it goes like this. How many counselors does it take to change a light bulb?" She waited for him to answer.

"I don't know."

"Only one, but it has to really want to change."

Kenny frowned. "I don't get it."

"That joke is funny to counselors, Kenny. It points out how hard it is to change or help someone if they don't want to be helped or changed. Of course, a light bulb can't want to change—only people can do that. Do you know why you hate to comb your hair, Kenny?"

Boy, Kenny thought. *She sure asks a lot of questions.* Out loud he said, "It's too much trouble. I mean, it always gets messed up again. Once you start combing your hair, there's no stopping." He leaned forward in his chair. "Why, my sister must comb her hair a million times a day!"

"I see. Let's try something else, Kenny. I want you to hold this stone"—Dr. Shoemaker picked up the round blue-green stone—"and make a wish. You may wish whatever you like, but you may only make one wish." She handed the stone to Kenny.

Kenny took the stone from her hand. It was heavy, much heavier than he expected and it was warm, almost hot. When Kenny looked very carefully, he thought he could see something inside the stone move. But the stone wasn't quite transparent enough to see into. It was sort of smoky. "Make a wish. Are you serious?" he asked.

"Oh, yes, I'm serious. This is a very special stone. Your wish will come true, so wish carefully."

Weird, Kenny thought. He decided to humor Dr. Shoemaker and get the visit over with. "Umm, okay." He spoke quickly, "I wish, I wish I really had wild hair. Then my parents would be sorry they made such a fuss over my slightly messy hair." Kenny handed the stone to Dr. Shoemaker. She laid it back on her desk. With both hands, Kenny reached up and felt his hair. It didn't feel any different, but he felt foolish.

"Kenny," Dr. Shoemaker said. He jumped and put his hands in his lap. "Do you want to start combing your hair, Kenny?"

"No. I like it this way."

"Well, Kenny, you have to want to change before I can help you." She stood up. "Do you have any questions, Kenny?"

Kenny also stood up. "That's it? You mean I don't have hairphobia or something?" he asked unbelievingly.

"I've never heard of it, Kenny, but now that you mention it, you may have a very slight case." Dr. Shoemaker laughed. "I think you'll outgrow it. Come see me anytime, that is, anytime you're willing to change your attitude toward hair combing. Good-bye, Kenny."

"Good-bye, Dr. Shoemaker," he said and hesitated. "Dr. Shoemaker?"

"Yes, Kenny."

"Will my wish really come true?"

"Oh, yes. It will, Kenny, soon."

Kenny Bigfoot-walked back to his classroom. He didn't really believe wishes came true. Only little kids believed that.

Chapter
Eight / Love
Hurts

"Mrs. Welty." Kenny, standing outside his classroom door, heard his teacher's name called from inside the room.

"Mrs. Welty!" He heard her name called again, louder and whinier. It was Donald Sims, the class know-it-all. Donald always tried to run everything.

"Yes, Donald," Mrs. Welty answered, "what is it this time?"

"May I show Matthew how to do the math problems? They're way too hard for him. He doesn't even know how to get started."

"I do so! Mrs. Welty, I don't want him to help me," Matthew wailed.

"Donald," Mrs. Welty said slowly and tiredly, "when I die, I may will this classroom to you or I may not. However, until I die I am the boss, not you. MYOB. Mind Your Own Business."

On the last class field trip, a hike to a pond

to study aquatic life, everyone wore backpacks filled with their lunch and notebooks. Everyone except Donald. His backpack was filled with a first-aid kit and towels in case someone got hurt.

Kenny opened the door, walked in and sat at his desk. Mrs. Welty smiled at him. Kenny had stopped Bigfoot-walking as soon as he reached the classroom door. Unlike substitutes, Mrs. Welty knew exactly what to do with Bigfoot-walkers.

The last time she caught Kenny Bigfooting, she took him out in the hall and stood him against a wall. "Kenny," she said, "I've told you and told you not to walk that way. Now you're going to stand against this wall until you turn into a fossil." Her favorite subject was science.

His legs did feel like stone by the time Mrs. Welty said, "You may come back in the room and sit down, Kenny." After that, he decided never to Bigfoot-walk again, at least not in front of Mrs. Welty.

He had a good seat this year. It was close to the back of the room. Pete's desk was at his right side. Krista Bennett, the new girl, sat two seats up from Pete's desk. Krista had moved into Kenny's classroom one week ago. Cindy March, the prettiest girl in the room before Krista moved in, sat behind Kenny.

Kenny never took much notice of girls before Krista, but she was special. He opened his reading book and pretended to be reading but was really looking at Krista. She bent over her desk, writing on a piece of paper attached to her clear acrylic clipboard. Her name, in dot lettering, was painted in blue across the top of the clipboard.

Little blue paint flowers danced around her name. Krista's name was also dot-lettered on her lunchbox, her backpack, her pencils and her Thermos.

Since Krista's arrival, lots of girls in the room owned a clipboard, with their name dot-lettered across the top. Of course, not everyone liked Krista. Some of the kids thought she was stuck up. They called her "slimer, the perfect image of snot."

Everything Krista owned was beautiful, especially her clothes. Actually, her clothes weren't just clothes. They were outfits. Everything matched. Today she had on a pink sweatshirt and black jeans. She wore a necklace of pink and black beads under the black collar of the sweatshirt. Lots of little tan bears, dressed in white leotards and black socks, were doing exercises all over the front and back of the sweatshirt. Krista's pink socks matched the sweatshirt. Black sneakers completed her outfit.

Kenny stared openly at Krista as she walked to the front of the room to sharpen her pencil. His adoration was interrupted by Cindy March. "Psst, Kenny," Cindy whispered, "Krista wants to talk to you at lunch. Okay?"

Kenny smiled and nodded. *Okay*, Kenny thought, *it was more than okay, it was wonderful. Krista likes me! She wants to eat lunch with me.* He couldn't wait until lunchtime. *I'm gonna ask her to meet me at the skating rink Friday night. If she does, I'm gonna ask her to go with me. This is great!*

The skating rink, on Friday nights, was the place for fifth-grade courtship. Pete had already gone with eight girls this year. He went skating a lot. Krista would be the first for Kenny. Not just the first this year, the first ever.

Kenny's class ate lunch at 12:25. At 12:20, Mrs. Welty said, "All right, class, lunchtime. No, Donald, you may not be line leader. Lunchbox people, you may line up." She waited for them to grab their lunches from under their desks and get in line. "No, Donald, I did not forget. It's tomorrow, not today, that lunchbox people line up last. Salad bar people, you may line up." She waited again, then continued. "Regular line people, you may line up." When the noise died down she said, "All right, let's go. Quietly, people. No talking in the hall. No, Donald, you may not take the names of the people who talk in the hall."

The class trooped down the hall to the cafeteria. By the time Kenny got his tray from the regular line, Krista, a lunchbox person, was eating. Girls sat at her left and right, but the seat across from her was empty.

Proudly, Kenny took his tray of tacos and a cinnamon roll over to her table. He stood in front of Krista, looking around and smiling, hoping everyone noticed he was about to eat lunch with her. He thought about dropping his tray, to attract attention, but decided that wouldn't be cool. As he sat down, Krista and the girls stopped talking. Silently, they all stared across the table at Kenny. "Hi, Krista," he said and smiled. "I hear you want to have lunch with me."

The girls burst into a giggling fit. "Who told you that?" Krista asked between giggles.

"Well, Cindy did. She gave me your message," Kenny said, suddenly feeling foolish. He picked up his fork and filled it with corn, the savory vegetable of the day. As he moved the fork toward his mouth, most of the grains of corn rolled off onto his lap. One of them rolled across the table and hit Krista's sandwich.

"I did not!" Cindy said crossly. "Krista, I never said you wanted to have lunch with him. I said you wanted to talk to him at lunch."

"It's all right," Krista said. "Listen, Kenny, you're Pete's best friend, right?" Kenny nodded. "Well, I want you to ask him to meet me at the skating rink Friday night." She giggled again. "He's real cute, but I don't know if he likes me. If he meets me, I want to ask him to go with me. If I can get up the nerve. Would you ask him for me, if he'll meet me? Ask him today and tell Cindy what he says. She'll tell me. Okay?"

Miserably, Kenny nodded again. "Sure, Krista," he said, managing a weak smile, "will do." He stood up. Corn fell from his lap onto the floor, but he didn't notice. He took his full tray over to the garbage cans, dumped it and went back to his classroom.

Later that day, at recess, Kenny and Pete were goofing around with a soccer ball, bouncing it off their knees, back and forth to each other. Kenny decided to get it over with. "Hey, Pete, Krista wants to know if you'll meet her at the skating rink Friday night. She thinks you're cute. She wants to go with you. I'm supposed to ask you and tell Cindy what you say."

"Can't," Pete said as he caught the soccer ball. "I'm meeting Misty Hull. We're going together. I thought you liked Krista."

"She's okay."

After recess, when Kenny's class was back in their seats, quietly working, a piece of paper fell on Kenny's desk. He looked up in time to see Cindy walking to the pencil sharpener. Kenny picked up the paper. It was folded twice. A flower was drawn on one side. Beneath the flower was written, "For Kenny Wild's eyes only. TOP SECRET. From Cindy."

Kenny opened the paper and read, "Will he or won't he?" Kenny wrote, "He won't," refolded the paper and handed it to Cindy as she walked back by his desk. It was a long afternoon for Kenny. When the last bell finally rang, he picked up his books and headed for home, head hanging so low his chin rested on his chest.

Chapter
Nine / Cooking
with Kenny

Kenny walked home slowly. He knew lots of questions were in store for him once his parents got home. After dinner, if they could wait that long, his parents would take Kenny into the living room for a little parent-to-son chat. "So, Kenny," they would say, "how did it go with Dr. Shoemaker today?" Right now, he was too sad to have a parent-to-son chat.

Once home, Kenny went straight to the kitchen. He and Valerie had kitchen chores tonight. Kenny would cook and Valerie would clean up. Sometimes, when he cooked alone, Kenny liked to pretend he was the star of his own TV cooking show. That evening, the kitchen became his television studio.

"Hello, ladies and gentlemen," he said, smiling broadly into Camera One as he tied an apron around his waist. Kenny stood behind the kitchen counter, facing the studio audience. Actually, he was facing the kitchen table. He pretended Camera One was on his left and Camera Two was on his right. "Welcome to 'Cooking With Kenny.' Tonight's menu is a real treat, pepperoni pizza, garlic bread, chocolate ice cream and tossed green salad. I call it Dinner à la Freezer."

He turned to face Camera Two. "Frozen pizza is my family's favorite dinner." He paused to smile. "They like it because it tastes good. I like it because it's easy to fix after a hard day at school. All the cook has to do is read and follow the directions on the back of the box."

Kenny walked over to the refrigerator, took a frozen pizza and a loaf of bread from the freezer and carried them back to the counter. He turned to face Camera Two and smiled. "The only tricky part is remembering to remove the pizza from the box before placing it in the oven—the pizza, that is, not the box."

He smiled into Camera Two again before opening the box, taking the pizza from the box, putting it on a pizza pan and bending over to put it in the oven. When he bent over, the pizza slid off the pan, onto the floor. "Oops!" Kenny exclaimed, picking up the pizza. He wiped the back of it across his pants legs a couple of times, put it back on the pan and put it in the oven. He closed the oven door and turned to face Camera One. He smiled. "That's a special thing I always do to give the pizza more flavor. It's my little secret. Don't tell my family."

Still facing Camera One, he said, "The garlic bread is easy too." He paused and picked up the loaf of bread he had taken from the freezer. He held it up for the studio audience to see. "Just make sure you buy bread that's already buttered, garlicked and sliced. Then all you have to do is stick it in the oven with the pizza."

He did, but only after dropping the loaf and stepping on it. He dropped it behind the counter, out of camera range, so he pretended it hadn't happened. The loaf was frozen, so being stepped on didn't hurt it.

"Chocolate ice cream for dessert is easy too. Just keep it frozen until dessert time, then dish it out. It's the tossed green salad that takes the most time."

He walked over to the refrigerator again. This time he got a head of iceberg lettuce from the crisper, carried it over to the studio and set it on the kitchen counter. He turned to face Camera Two and smiled.

"I always begin a salad by decoring the lettuce. No, not decorating, decoring—taking the core out. Once the core is out, the head of lettuce is easy to rip apart. This is the best way to do it. Watch closely. It's a neat trick, ladies and gentlemen. You won't see this on any other show."

Kenny took a deep breath and grabbed the head of lettuce firmly in both hands. Making sure the core pointed downward, he smashed the lettuce head several times against the counter.

He stopped smashing, looked up into Camera Two and said, "You've got to smash really hard. It helps to pretend the lettuce is someone you're mad at, like Krista Bennett." He smashed some more. After ten or so vigorous smashes, Kenny felt better, less depressed. He stopped smashing and turned the lettuce so the core faced upward. "Now, the core should lift out easily. If it doesn't, you didn't smash hard enough and you need to try again."

Kenny was trying again when his parents got home from work and walked into the kitchen. "So, Kenny, how did it go with Dr. Shoemaker today?" his dad asked.

By now, Kenny felt good, giddy and reckless. "She said I may have a mild case of hairphobia, but it's just something I'm growing through." He giggled. "It's nothing to worry about."

His parents looked at each other, turned and walked out of the kitchen. Kenny finished the salad, set the table and called everyone to dinner.

While the family ate dinner, no one said anything about Kenny's hair or Dr. Shoemaker. Mrs. Wild helped Kenny dish out the chocolate ice cream. "Kenny," she said, "your dad and I are going to say one more thing about your hair, then we're going to drop it. We won't ever mention hair again and you won't either." She looked at him seriously and asked, "Promise?"

"Promise," Kenny replied, scratching a tiny bump on his left cheek. *Great, no more nagging*, he thought.

"Kenny, comb your hair, or one day you'll be sorry."

"That's it? That's all you're going to say about my hair?"

"Yes."

Kenny finished eating and watched TV while Valerie cleaned up. Later, he did his homework, said good night to his parents and went to bed. When Kenny left for school the next morning, his hair was as wild as ever. His parents seemed not to notice and said nothing about his hair.

Chapter
Ten / The Beard

"Go on! Do it!" Pete yelled.

"Come on, do it!" Kenny shouted.

"Do it, Willie! Hurry up," Kenny's whole class screamed at once. Kenny's PE class was playing volleyball in the school cafeteria. If it rained or was too cold to go outside, PE had to be inside, but the school had no gym. The cafeteria was the best indoors place to have PE. It was a rainy day and two classes were having PE at once. Sixty screaming voices bounced off the concrete walls and floor of the school cafeteria.

Kenny was lucky. He had PE early in the morning, before the cafeteria had to be cleared for lunch. PE classes that met from 10:30 to 1:30 had to be held in a regular classroom. It's hard to play volleyball in a room full of desks. For those classes Mr. Pumice, the PE teacher, "Coach" to his students, usually did something he called "Plan B." Kenny knew that was just a fancy name for dumb old word-search puzzles.

"Cheez, Snotnose, do it already. Just hit it," Pete yelled. He was captain of the receiving team.

Across the net, Willie "Snotnose" Gunder stood holding the volleyball. He had been holding it a long time. He looked scared. It was his turn to serve. He was terrible at serving. He never got the ball over the net. He tucked the ball under his left arm and wiped his nose with the back of his right hand. Willie's nose always needed wiping. That's why his classmates called him Snotnose Willie, or sometimes just Snotnose. Coach didn't like the class to call Willie "Snotnose." He said Willie couldn't help it if he had allergies that made his nose run. Of course, Coach never had to eat lunch sitting across the table from Willie.

When Willie heard his hated nickname, he held the ball up in his left hand, and closed his eyes. He drew his right arm way back, brought it forward and smacked the volleyball as hard as he could. The ball flew into the air, over the net, straight for the receiving team. The whole PE class went crazy. Even Pete's team jumped up and down, clapped their hands and screamed and cheered. Pete's team was still screaming and jumping when the ball landed. It was in bounds. After three weeks of volleyball, Snotnose Willie got the ball over the net.

"Good going, Willie," Coach said. "All right class, line up. Time to go back to Mrs. Welty. No Donald, you may not tell her Pete said the 'S' word." Mrs. Welty also didn't like the class to call Willie "Snotnose."

Pete got in line behind Kenny. "Hey, Kenny, what's that?" he asked and pointed.

Kenny knew Pete was pointing at the little black hair on his left cheek. "Oh, you mean this hair?" he asked innocently, pooching out his cheek with his tongue and pointing with one finger. "That's just my beard. It's already started to grow. I woke up this morning, and there it was. Yesterday it was just a little bump."

"Cool," Pete said. "Don't you wish we had a real gym with showers and lockers and everything, so everybody could watch you shave?"

Kenny hadn't actually started to shave. He only had one little short black hair, but he didn't want to lose a chance to show off. "Yeah," he agreed. "That'd be great. Why don't you come over after school and I'll let you watch me shave." Kenny forgot all about being grounded.

"Okay, but shave at my house. My parents won't mind."

"Okay."

The class marched back to Mrs. Welty's room. "Mrs. Welty! Mrs. Welty!" Donald yelled the instant he saw his teacher, "Pete said the 'S' word in PE."

Chapter Eleven / The Close Shave

After school, Pete and Kenny walked to Pete's house. They had a quick snack of Ding Dongs and milk, then went to Pete's room. They fed a leaf of lettuce to Houdini, Pete's hamster. Kenny stuck one hand inside Houdini's cage and stroked his soft furry side. "Has Houdini escaped again?"

"Not since we got the mesh cage."

When Pete first got his hamster, he named him Hercules and kept him in a regular wire cage, the kind with little vertical bars. The first night, Pete told Hercules good night and covered his cage. The next morning, when Pete uncovered the cage, it was empty. Pete searched and searched but couldn't find Hercules. Pete's mom found him when she was getting dressed to go to work. She was all ready, except for her shoes. Luckily, she wasn't the sort of person who jammed her feet into her shoes. She really screamed when her toes touched fur.

Pete took Hercules out of his mother's shoe and put him back in his cage. The next morning the cage was once again empty. Pete's mom made the whole family search for Hercules. She claimed she couldn't get dressed in the mornings until he was found. They searched and searched but couldn't find the hamster. Pete finally decided Hercules got outside somehow and was gone forever. For the next three mornings, Pete's mom turned her shoes upside down and shook them before putting them on. Then Sammy found Hercules.

Sammy was looking through the kitchen cabinets for a box of Kraft macaroni and cheese, but he found Hercules. Somehow the hamster had fallen inside a large glass pitcher and couldn't climb up its smooth slippery sides. Hercules was fine, hungry but fine.

After those two great escapes, Pete changed Hercules's name to Houdini, after the great magician and escape artist. Pete also kept Houdini's cage in the bathtub at night until he could buy an escape-proof hamster cage.

"Ready to shave?" Pete asked Kenny.

"Sure," Kenny replied. "I'm ready anytime."

Pete opened his bedroom door, stuck his head out and peeked up and down the hall. He looked left and right many times. He saw the bathroom door was open and that the coast was clear. He pulled his head back inside and turned to face Kenny. "Okay," he whispered. "Don't say a word until we're inside the bathroom. We'll be safe from him in there. Let's go."

They tippy-toed down the hall to the bathroom, trying to avoid Sammy, Pete's stinky little brother. Sammy's favorite pastime was following Pete and Kenny around, trying to do whatever they did. His mother thought Sammy was wonderful. She never got onto Sammy for bothering Pete.

Kenny and Pete arrived safely at the bathroom door. They locked the door as soon as they were inside. Pete walked over to the medicine cabinet. "Here's my dad's razor," he said, holding out a throwaway plastic razor. "And here's my dad's shaving cream. And here's—say, do you hear something?"

Kenny listened for a moment. "No, I don't. Do you?"

"I thought I heard a crunchy noise. Did you step on something?"

Kenny looked down at his feet. "No." He looked back up. "Come on, Pete. Stop fooling around. Give me that stuff. Let's get this show on the road." Kenny shook the can of shaving cream. Holding it next to his cheek, he looked in the mirror, trying to find the little hair. He wanted to squirt the shaving cream right on the hair. He found the hair, he aimed and he started to squeeze the nozzle. He heard something. "I hear something!" he shouted and dropped the can. "It's a crunchy noise. Listen!"

They stood very still and listened.

"Crunch."

The crunch sound was coming from the bathtub. The shower curtain hid whatever was making the noise.

"Crunch, crunch, crunch." The sound grew louder and louder.

"Go look," Pete said.

"You go look, it's your house!" Kenny remembered all the horror movies he'd seen where things hid in your bathtub. It was probably a giant rat, eating Wooter, Pete's dog. No way was he going to look.

"Okay, chicken." Pete said. "I'll go." He started toward the tub, stopped and picked up the can of shaving cream. He placed one finger on the nozzle and pointed it toward the tub. He moved toward the tub again, ready to shoot whatever was in there.

"Crunch, crunch."

"Wait," Kenny said. "I can't let you do this

alone. I'll whip the shower curtain back. You blast whatever's in there." He stood by the bathtub and put one hand on the shower curtain, ready to whip it back. "On the count of three, I whip, you blast. Ready? One, two, three!"

He jerked the curtain back. Kenny and Pete stared open-mouthed at the thing in the tub. It was a giant rat. It was Sammy.

"Maconie?" Sammy asked sweetly. He stood in the tub, holding an open box of Kraft macaroni-and-cheese. He dipped one hand into the box, grabbed several macaronis and stuffed them into his mouth. "Crunch, crunch," he chewed, smiled and shook the box at them. Some of the macaroni fell into the tub.

Macaroni-and-cheese was Sammy's favorite food in the whole world. He loved it raw or cooked. The rest of his family only liked it cooked. Mrs. Williams smuggled it into the house and hid it from Sammy, until she was ready to cook it. She didn't like him to eat it raw.

"You little jerk! You creep! I oughta blast you anyway," Pete yelled, but he put the shaving cream down. "Now get out of here and leave us alone or I'll tell Mom to find a new hiding place for your old macaroni."

"I go," Sammy said. He tried, but he couldn't climb out of the tub. "Help Sammy go," he pleaded.

"No. Come on, Kenny. Let's leave the little creep in there. If he can't get out of the tub, he can't bother us. It's the perfect babysitter." Shaving forgotten, they went back to Pete's room. They left Sammy in the tub, happily munching his "maconie."

"Whew," Kenny said, "that was a close shave."

"Kenny!" Mrs. Williams yelled from the kitchen. She avoided Pete's room whenever possible. "Your mother just phoned. She wants me to remind you that you're grounded. You're not to go anywhere but home and school. She wants you home right now."

"Grounded!" Kenny exclaimed and slapped his forehead. "I forgot. I'll probably get another week for this. I gotta go. See ya tomorrow."

Chapter
Twelve / The Vow
of Silence

At school the next day, Kenny sat at his desk and fidgeted. He found it hard to sit still. He felt sort of itchy all over. Strangely enough, the part of him that itched the most was the roof of his mouth. Kenny tried to scratch it with his tongue, but that didn't help. He noticed the roof of his mouth felt bumpy. He squirmed in his seat, "Psst, Pete," Kenny said. Actually, he whispered because he was talking to Pete during math, whenever Mrs. Welty wasn't looking.

Pete looked up from his math work. "What?" he whispered back.

"Mom didn't ground me for another week. She said she would overlook it this time, since I ran home right after she called. And she said I can walk to school with you or home with you."

"That's good. Can I come over after school? I could watch you shave at your house."

"No, she said no visits, just the walks. I can't have friends over when I'm grounded. Besides, I don't have anything to shave. I woke up this morning and the hair was gone."

Their talk was stopped by their teacher. "All right, Kenny. You lose half your recess time for talking in math. I've given you forewarning about that talking. It's got to stop," Mrs. Welty said crossly.

Kenny was indignant. He shot back a reply, "Four warnings! You never gave me four warnings. This is the first time today you've said anything about talking. That's not fair."

"No, no, Kenny. I said forewarning, not four warnings. Forewarning means—oh, never mind. You've still lost half your recess time, and Pete, you lose half your time."

Kenny and Pete spent half their recess standing against one wall of the school building. Kenny was angry. Mrs. Welty was mean and unfair. Standing still was almost as hard as sitting still.

After recess, back in the classroom, Kenny fidgeted and squirmed. He felt itchier than ever. Finally, the dismissal bell rang. Kenny and Pete walked home together. "Boy, Mrs. Welty sure was mean to us today," Kenny said.

"Yeah," Pete agreed. "She's the meanest teacher in the whole world."

"That's right, she is. When I was little, I got mad at my mom, ran out to the garage and locked myself in our car. I wish I could do something like that to Mrs. Welty." Kenny paused, then added, "Mom never did come looking for me."

That night, Kenny went to sleep still angry. The next morning, half asleep, he walked into the bathroom to get ready for another day with the meanest teacher in the world. Sleepily, he stood in front of the bathroom sink, picked up his toothbrush and opened his mouth. As soon as he opened his mouth, out popped a hair. It was a long, curly black hair and it was growing from the roof of his mouth.

Kenny was wide awake now. He stuffed the hair back inside his mouth. He opened his mouth just a tiny bit and out popped the hair. He stuffed it back inside his mouth. He tried to say, "Good morning, Mrs. Welty," but the hair popped out before he said, "Good." He stuffed it back in, filled a paper cup with water and started to take a sip. The hair popped out again. He stuffed it back inside his mouth. The hair felt terrible, but if he kept his mouth shut it stayed put.

You might as well face it, he thought, *you're not opening your mouth the rest of the day. It's going to be tough getting through a day in the life of Kenny Wild without talking. But you can't tell your parents. You promised not to mention hair. Oh no, what am I going to do at school? How can I face the meanest teacher in the world without being able to talk all day?*

He walked over to his desk, took a sheet of paper from his notebook and began to write. *I may not be able to lock myself in Mrs. Welty's car,* he thought, *but I can do something almost as good.* When he finished, he folded the paper, put it in his shirt pocket and went downstairs.

"Good morning, Kenny," his mother said when he walked into the kitchen. Kenny grunted and sat down at the kitchen table.

"Hey, Potato Face," Valerie said. Kenny looked down at the table. "Hey, Kenny," Valerie tried again. Kenny kept staring at the table. "Hey, creep! Hey Nerd Face. I'm talking to you!" she yelled.

He looked at her. Valerie wore his new green sweatshirt. She had changed the sweatshirt so it would match her new blue jeans, which didn't look new. Her jeans had ragged slits instead of knees and were so faded they were almost white. His sweatshirt no longer looked new. The neck band and one sleeve band were torn completely off. The other sleeve was cut off at the elbow. Right in the middle of the front of the shirt was one large hole. The back had several small holes.

Kenny had only worn the shirt once. Now

it was ruined. His eyes bugged out. He longed to stick out his tongue, but he didn't dare. Valerie noticed his startled look, grinned and said, "Consider us even for Bob Stevens." She stood, picked up her books and walked toward the door. "I'm going, Mom. Bye."

"Kenny, do you want some breakfast?" Mrs. Wild asked.

Kenny shook his head. He did want breakfast but he couldn't eat without opening his mouth. He would have to do without food all day, maybe all week. He didn't know how long the hair would stay in his mouth. Maybe he could never eat again. Maybe he would starve to death. His stomach growled loudly, as if it hadn't been fed in days. Kenny felt very hungry.

"Are you sure? You really should eat something. Breakfast is the most important meal of the day." Kenny took the folded sheet of paper from his shirt pocket and handed it to his mother. "What's this, a note?" She opened the paper and read it. She started to say something, but smiled instead and refolded the note. "Well, good luck," she said and handed it to Kenny.

Kenny put the note back in his shirt pocket. It was a relief to leave for school and get away from the smell of food. Kenny walked by himself. Every few steps he checked his pocket to make sure his note was still there. Kenny sighed as he walked through the doors of Westdale Elementary. He knew it would be another long day.

Mrs. Welty was sitting at her desk, taking lunch money. Kenny walked up to her and handed her the note. As she read it to herself, she began to smile. She folded the note and rapped on her desk for attention. "Class, I have an important announcement to make. Kenny has just informed me that he has taken a vow of silence. It seems that he thinks his punishment for talking in class yesterday was unfair. He has decided to protest his punishment by not speaking to anyone for any reason, until further notice."

She was trying not to laugh, but the corners of her mouth kept twitching upward as she continued. "I'm sure this will be a terrible burden for all of us to bear. Please help Kenny keep his vow of silence. Don't try to make him talk. Is there anyone who would like to join Kenny in his protest?" she asked hopefully and paused. Pete raised his hand. "Very good, Pete. You too may protest your punishment by not talking. Kenny is also on a hunger strike. Would you like to join him in that too, Pete?

"No!" Pete exclaimed. "Oops!" He slapped

both hands over his mouth and shook his head.

"No? All right, class, you may continue with your work."

The vow of silence worked. Despite the best efforts of everyone in his class to get him to talk, he was able to keep his mouth shut all day. By the end of the day he was starving, but he didn't dare eat in front of anyone, which meant he couldn't eat at school. At Westdale, you were never alone, not even in the bathroom.

Not talking all day gave Kenny lots of time to think. Mostly he thought about Dr. Shoemaker and her stone. He was sure his wish on the stone was the cause of his problem. He had to talk to her, even if the hair popped out. When the dismissal bell rang, Kenny walked down the hall to Dr. Shoemaker's office. Taped to her door was a message, it said, "Dr. Shoemaker will not be in today (Thursday) or tomorrow (Friday). She will be in very early Monday morning."

Kenny turned away from her door and walked home. He was the first person home. He headed for the kitchen and pigged out on a quart of ice cream and three glasses of chocolate milk. Before he went upstairs to his room, he left a note on the kitchen table. The note said, "I'm lying down in my room. I don't feel so good." His stomach really did feel sick.

As soon as his mother got home and read his note she went to Kenny's room. He pretended to be asleep. She felt his forehead and tucked his arms under the covers, but she didn't try to wake him. After she left, Kenny really did fall asleep.

Chapter
Thirteen / The Walking
Sticker Album

Kenny woke up the next morning, and with his tongue felt the inside of his mouth. He didn't feel the hair. Joyfully, Kenny sprang out of bed and ran to the bathroom. He looked in the mirror and felt his stomach sink to his feet. The hair was right smack dab in the middle of his forehead! It was longer and curlier and blacker than before. Kenny groaned. How could he go to school with the hair in such a funny place? There was no way he could pass this hair off as part of a beard.

Kenny cut the hair off with scissors, but it grew back in an instant. He tried again, but it grew back longer and blacker and curlier. Kenny went back to his room to think. He paced around and around the room until he bumped into his desk. His sticker album lay open on top of his desk. Kenny knew what to do. He hoped Valerie wouldn't notice.

Kenny went downstairs to breakfast with

a large sticker in the middle of his forehead. He also wore stickers on his sleeves, shirt front and back and on his jeans.

As soon as he walked into the kitchen, Valerie burst out laughing. "Kenny," she gasped between laughs, "you're not going to school like that! You look silly. Mom, look at Kenny. Tell him he can't go to school wearing all those stickers, especially the one on his forehead."

"Val, eat your breakfast. I'll take care of Kenny. Kenny, I'm glad you feel well enough to go to school, but you're not going to school like that. You look ridiculous."

"Oh, Mom! All the kids at school are wearing stickers. We got tired of just putting them in sticker albums. It's cool to wear them, to be a walking sticker album. You don't want me to be a nerd, do you? I just gotta wear the stickers. Please, Mom, please, please." He fell to his knees, hands clasped in front of him. He put on his most pitiful look, the one he practiced in front of the mirror in case of emergencies like this one. It worked.

"All right, all right, Kenny. Wear the stupid things if it's that important to you. Your hair is so wild and funny looking, what difference can a few little stickers make? Oops, sorry, I forgot my promise. Just forget I mentioned hair. You go ahead, humiliate and embarrass your family again, who cares? I notice you're talking today. Are you eating, too?"

"Yeah."

"Fine, you know where the cereal is, help yourself. Why does your dad always leave for work before I do? Why couldn't he be here to deal with HIS son?" Kenny's mother didn't give in gracefully.

Kenny ate breakfast and walked to school. "Good morning, Mrs. Welty," Kenny said when he walked into his classroom. He sat down at his desk.

"Good morning, Kenny," Mrs. Welty said. She was writing and looking down at her desktop. "I notice you're speaking, so I assume your protest has ended." She looked at Kenny, paused and said, "What on earth are you wearing?" She stood and walked over to him. "Stickers! Why are you wearing stickers, Kenneth?" Mrs. Welty called him Kenneth when she was very upset with him.

"I'm a walking sticker album."

Mrs. Welty walked back to her desk and sat down. "Class, I have another announcement. Kenneth's vow of silence has ended. However, he is now a walking sticker album." Everyone looked at Kenny. The girls in the class giggled. "Now, let's all admire him for a few moments, then we'll get down to work and not mention stickers anymore today."

The girls giggled again. Pete reached over and pulled a sticker off Kenny's sleeve. He put the sticker on his cheek and glared at the gigglers. They stopped. By the end of the day, several boys in the class were wearing at least one sticker.

After school, grounded or not, Kenny took Pete to his room. He told Pete all about his visit with Dr. Shoemaker. Then Kenny took the sticker off his forehead. The hair was still curled in the middle of his forehead.

"Wow! Now that's wild hair," Pete exclaimed. "Let's try cutting it off."

"Won't work. I tried that," Kenny said.

"You mean this isn't the first day you've had this wild hair?"

"No, I've had it several days now. It keeps moving around. The first day it was on my cheek. I pretended it was my beard. I've never really shaved, you know."

"I know," Pete said. "I knew all along you never shaved, but it was fun pretending to shave that day at my house, except for Sammy."

"And yesterday the hair was inside my mouth. That's the real reason I took the vow of silence. Every time I opened my mouth, even a tiny bit, the hair popped out," Kenny said.

"I'm glad it moved to the outside of your face. Not talking all day was really hard. I wouldn't want to do that again. Have you tried pulling it out?"

"No! And I'm not going to, that would hurt."

"Let's try shaving it off," Pete suggested.

"Okay. Come on. This time we'll use my dad's shaving cream and razor."

Kenny put the sticker back on, just in case they met Valerie in the hall. They walked to the bathroom and took Mr. Wild's shaving cream and razor from the medicine cabinet. Kenny took the sticker off his forehead and carefully placed it on the toilet tank. He might need it again. Pete aimed, closed one eye and squirted the cream on Kenny's forehead. After wiping off the mirror, the sink, the wall and Kenny's face (except for his forehead), they were ready to use the razor.

"Hold still! I'm going to hurt you if you keep flinching. And unscrunch your face. It wrinkles your forehead when you scrunch your face like that."

"I can't. I'm afraid you'll slice my nose off. Here, give me the razor, let me do it. I can if I look in the mirror." Kenny took the razor and carefully shaved off the hair. It grew back before he could throw the cut one into the toilet. "See, Pete. It doesn't work any better than cutting it off, like I tried to do this morning. The same thing happened."

"What's this?" Pete asked, picking up the can from the edge of the bathtub.

"That's hair-removal cream. My mom and Val use it on their legs."

"So if it's okay for their legs it must be okay for your face. Try it," Pete urged.

"Okay." Kenny squirted the cream into his hand. He didn't want hair remover all over the mirror, sink and walls. He sure didn't want it in his eyes. He gently dabbed the cream on the hair and waited. The directions on the can promised instant results. It had no effect. "I give up. No matter what I do, nothing works," Kenny said sadly.

"Well, maybe when you wake up tomorrow the hair will have moved to a new place." Pete said cheerfully.

"Yeah, but it could be a worse place. If it does move, who knows where it will be? You'd better go. My parents should be home soon. Their grounding includes visitors. I'm not supposed to have any."

"Okay, come by Monday and walk me to school."

"Okay, will do. Bye, Pete."

Kenny wiped the hair-removal cream off his forehead with the back of one hand, covered the hair with the sticker and went downstairs. It was his night to fix dinner. Kenny fried hamburgers, heated two cans of Campbell's Vegetarian Vegetable Soup and opened a bag of Ruffles. He set the table and put all the fixings for hamburgers out. "Come and get it," he called. His family came in and sat down.

"Looks good, Kenny," his mother said.

"It smells delicious," his dad said, reaching for a hamburger bun. "You've made a wonderful din . . ." his dad looked at Kenny and stopped in midsentence. "What is that on your forehead?"

"It's a sticker. I'm a walking sticker album. Everybody at school is wearing stickers."

"Oh. Well, it looks a little strange, but it's better than streaking, like we did in my day."

"Dad! You didn't!" Valerie exclaimed.

Mrs. Wild laughed.

"Didn't what?" Kenny asked.

"Streak, run naked through a crowd. Like at a football game," Valerie explained. "We're studying the 'seventies in my government class."

"No. I didn't," Mr. Wild replied. His face was redder than the soup. He tried to change the subject. "This hamburger is delicious, Kenny. Good job."

Mrs. Wild decided to help her husband.

She turned to Valerie and asked, "How was your day? Anything unusual happen?"

"Okay, except for biology. We're dissecting cats. They are so gross. When we first got them, they were floating around inside plastic bags of formaldehyde. The smell when you open the bag is bad, real bad. I can still smell the formaldehyde on my hands. The whole thing is just too gross!"

"Cats. That's interesting," Mrs. Wild said. "When I took high school biology, we only dissected earthworms."

"My class did frogs," Mr. Wild said.

Oh great, Kenny thought. *They'll probably be dissecting horses by the time I take high school biology.*

The hair stayed on Kenny's forehead all weekend. He kept it covered with the sticker. By Sunday, most of the sticky stuff was worn off the sticker. He had to use Enduro Superstick to glue it to his forehead.

Chapter
Fourteen / Dr. Shoemaker Returns

On Monday morning Kenny rushed to the bathroom and pulled the sticker off his forehead. "Ouch! That Enduro stuff works better on skin than glass." Only half the sticker came off. He used a cotton ball soaked in nail polish remover to get the rest off. When the sticker was all gone, he looked in the mirror. His face was smooth and hairless, even his forehead. "What a relief!"

He pulled his pajama top over his head. His mouth fell open when he saw the hair growing on his stomach, right above his belly button. It was longer and curlier and blacker than ever. *Calm down, calm down,* he thought. *This isn't so bad. You can hide it under your shirt.* Kenny dressed and went downstairs. He kept his left hand on his stomach, on top of the hair. He didn't want to take any chances. The hair might pop out between the buttons of his shirt.

"Good morning, Mom. Good morning, Valerie," he said cheerfully, as he walked into the kitchen. He was going to make the best of this day, in spite of the hair.

"Good morning, Kenny," his mother said. "I hear you're still talking. Want some breakfast?"

"Good morning, twerp," Valerie said sweetly.

"Yeah, but I'll fix it."

He walked over to the Wheaties box. One-handed, he poured cereal into a bowl and added milk. One-handed, he picked up a spoon and the full bowl of cereal and carried them to the table. One-handed, he set the bowl and spoon on the table, pulled out a chair, sat down and began to eat.

"Does your stomach hurt? Or are you just afraid I'm going to punch you?" Valerie asked.

"It's none of your business if my stomach hurts, Valerie."

"Most normal people don't walk around clutching their stomachs for no reason. Of course you're not, by any stretch of the imagination, a normal person."

"Does your stomach hurt, Kenny?" his mother asked.

"No, Mom. I feel great today. Where's Dad?" he asked, trying to change the subject. He took his left hand off his stomach. *Guess*

I'll just have to risk it popping out, he thought.

"He left early again. He claims he has a report due, but I think he leaves early so he can drive around in his new car before he goes to the office."

Kenny ate quickly. "Bye. I'm gonna go see Pete, before school."

He walked over to Pete's house and knocked. Pete answered the door, looked at Kenny's forehead and said, "Great, the hair's gone. See, I told you it would move. What's up?"

"I've got to talk to Dr. Shoemaker alone. I can't wait for you."

"Dr. Shoemaker, huh? Is that about the hair? Is it driving you crazy? Where is it today?"

Kenny unbuttoned his shirt and showed Pete the hair on his stomach. "Yeah, it's about the hair. See ya at school."

"See ya, Kenny. Don't do anything stupid."

Kenny walked straight to the counselor's office and knocked on her door. "Come in, Kenny." Kenny opened the door and walked inside the room. "Hello, Kenny. Won't you sit down?" Dr. Shoemaker asked, pointing to the chair across from her desk.

"How did you know it was me?" Kenny asked as he sat down.

"Oh, I had a hunch you'd be back to see me. How can I help you today, Kenny?"

Kenny unbuttoned his shirt. "Look," he demanded and pointed at the hair.

"I see," said Dr. Shoemaker. "So your wish came true, Kenny."

"I didn't wish for this kind of wild hair. I've had it several days now and every day it's in a different place. I wished for wild hair on my head, like David Dude's hair."

"Wishes don't always turn out the way we expect, Kenny."

"Your stupid stone put it there and I want it off! I take back my wish!"

"How do you think the stone put it there, Kenny?"

"The wish, the stupid wish you had me make last time I was here. Where did you get that stone? You should throw it away. It's magic and it's dangerous!"

"Well, Kenny, to make a long story short, it was a gift from a swami who lives in India. It is a magic stone, but once a wish has been made, it can't be unwished. But all that doesn't really matter, Kenny."

Kenny decided she must have gone to a workshop that trained counselors to call people by their name three hundred times in three minutes.

"What matters, Kenny, is you. Are you

ready to change, Kenny? Do you want to start combing your 'slightly messy' hair?"

"No! Yes! I mean yes and no. Yes, I want to change by getting rid of this wild hair. No, I don't want to start combing my slightly messy hair. It's important to me and I want to keep it."

"Kenny, only you can get rid of your wild hair. But in order to get rid of it you have to find something you want more, something that is more important to you than your 'slightly messy' hair."

"Okay," Kenny said glumly, "thanks." *Thanks for nothing*, he thought. He Bigfooted it back to his classroom and sat at his desk just as the tardy bell rang.

"Psst, Kenny," Pete hissed. "How did it go with Dr. Shoemaker? Did she help?" Talking after the tardy bell rang was forbidden. If caught, they would spend time against the wall at recess.

"No." Kenny whispered. "I've still got the hair."

"This should cheer you up. Look at Donald."

Kenny looked over at Donald and grinned. Donald wore a sticker on the tip of his nose. Kenny was still grinning as he turned his head toward Krista's desk. She glanced over at him, smiled and turned away.

Boy, Kenny thought, *she sure is beautiful. It sure would be great if she liked me.* Kenny picked up his pencil and began working on that morning's chalkboard assignments.

Chapter
Fifteen / The Great
Cure Search

"Time for library, class. Put your pencils down," Mrs. Welty said. Donald raised his hand. "Yes, Donald?" Mrs. Welty asked.

"Can I call the rows?"

"May I, not can I. No, Donald, you may not call the rows. I will. Monday's row can get in line, now Tuesday's row, Wednesday's row, Thursday's row and Friday's. No, Donald," she said, before he could raise his hand, "you may not be line leader. Just stay where you are. You may go, class. I'll see you in thirty minutes."

Mrs. Welty smiled broadly as she watched her class march off to the library. She loved the planning time library class gave her. Kenny suspected she spent the time in the lounge, planning with other teachers fiendish ways to be mean to kids.

"Psst, Pete," Kenny whispered. "I need your help when we get to the library."

"Help with what?" Pete whispered back.

"Maybe there's a book that will tell me how to get rid of the hair."

"Good idea. We'll look in the card catalog."

The class marched down the hall and into the library media center.

"Good morning, boys and girls," Mrs. Sears, the media specialist, said. "Today is book checkout day. You have fifteen minutes to check out a book. Then we'll have a short lesson on using computers. Go ahead and check out now. Just give a yell if you need any help."

Pete and Kenny walked over to the card catalog. "What should we look under?" Pete asked.

"Let's try hair. I don't want anyone but you to know about this, so don't ask Mrs. Sears for help." They opened the "H" drawer and looked behind the "Ha" guide card for subject cards that had "HAIR" on the top line. "Here's one. It says, 'see Human Body, see also Folk Medicine.' Which should we look under?" Kenny asked.

"Try Human Body. We are interested in getting rid of human hair. And we're already in the "H" drawer." They looked behind the "Hu" guide card and found about a million cards with HUMAN BODY on the top line. Only one read: HUMAN BODY—HAIR. The title of the book was *Beauty School Dropout*.

"That's not what we need. Let's try Folk Medicine," Kenny said.

In the "F" drawer, they found only one subject card with "FOLK MEDICINE—HAIR" on the top line. It looked like this:

FOLK MEDICINE—HAIR

616
Cas   Caster, Mary.
      Rub it on or swallow it/by
Mary Caster. —Hardrock, AR:
Hardrock Press, 1985.
      178 p. : ill.
      Summary: More than 800 cures and remedies using natural re- sources.
      1. Folk Medicine— I. Title

"*Rub It on or Swallow It*. That sounds like what we need. Write the call number down, Pete. It's 616 Cas. Let's go find the book."

"Wait at that table. I'll bring it over," Pete said.

Pete found the book and took it over to Kenny. They turned to the back of the book and looked in the index. Hair was listed on pages 95–6. They turned to page 95, the beginning of a chapter titled, "Cures for What Ails You."

Pete read out loud, " 'Hot gooey onion poultices, placed on the chest, opens stuffy noses and makes breathing easier.' "

"That sounds stinky, and gross."

Pete read the next cure. " 'Cover your face with cow manure, leave it on until it dries, and your freckles will disappear.' "

"Your freckles and your friends," Kenny joked. "That's even stinkier. What's the next one?"

" 'Rub tobacco leaves on your skin and wear some in your underwear to keep insects away,' " Pete read. "I don't have insects in my underwear. You read the next one."

Kenny read, " 'Wear a freshly killed, cut-open frog on each elbow or knee that is aching from rheumatism. The ache will vanish.' "

"Super gross!" Pete exclaimed. "All the best-dressed kids are wearing frogs on their elbows, I'm sure. Listen to this one. 'Rub a dirty sock, the dirtier the better, on your neck to prevent sore throats. Then wear the sock on a string around your neck.' "

"I've got lots of dirty socks under my bed. Next time I have a sore throat, I might wear one around my neck instead of on my feet," Kenny said. "I'm almost afraid to ask, but aren't there any cures for wild hair?"

"Here's something about hair. 'Eating bread crusts or carrots makes hair curly.' "

"Sounds like a big story to get kids to eat bread crusts and carrots."

"Here's another one." Pete read, " 'To prevent headaches, never let a bird use any of your hair for its nest. Human hair in a bird's nest causes the hair's original owners to have a terrible headache.' "

"This is all very funny, but useless. Isn't there anything else on hair?"

Pete turned the page. "One more," he replied. "Listen, you're gonna love this one. 'To remove unwanted hair: Find a dead cat. Rub the cat over the hair and say, hair, hair go away, don't come again any day. Then bury the cat in your backyard, in the light of the moon. The hair will vanish within six hours.' "

"Let me see that." Kenny grabbed the book from Pete and read the cure. "You weren't kidding! This book really says to rub a dead cat on yourself."

"I know," Pete said and grinned.

"That's the worst one yet. I'd rather have the hair than rub a dead cat on me. Besides, where could we get a dead cat?" Kenny slammed the book shut. "This was a bad idea.

Put this back and let's check out a good book."

"I'll copy the cure first, just in case you change your mind."

Kenny checked out a joke book and Pete found a new book on monsters. The class had their lesson on computers and Mrs. Sears sent them back to Mrs. Welty.

"Take out your math books," Mrs. Welty said. She wasn't smiling anymore. "We're going to review multiplying decimals. Some of you didn't do too well on the last test." Kenny groaned and opened his math book. An eternity later Mrs. Welty said, "Close your books. It's time for PE." She smiled as she called the rows for lineup.

Time for more fiendish plots, Kenny thought as he got in line.

Kenny made it through the rest of the school day without the hair popping out from between his buttons,

Chapter
Sixteen / Hop-Along
Kenny

The next morning, when Kenny woke up, he felt his stomach. It was smooth and hairless. He touched the roof of his mouth. It was hair free. He touched his forehead and cheeks. They were smooth and hairless. "Whew! What a relief! I guess a wish can be unwished. Dr. Shoemaker doesn't know everything." He had to share the good news with Pete. Kenny whistled his favorite Skulls hit, "Santa Claus Skipped My Town," as he threw back the covers.

He sat up and put his feet on the floor. His right foot sprang up toward the ceiling. His left foot stayed on the floor. He tried putting his right foot down again. BOING! Back toward the ceiling it sprang. "What is going on?" He put his right foot down again and pressed hard on his knee to keep his foot on the floor. "Gee, the floor feels funny. Maybe it's time to vacuum in here," he mumbled. "Unless, oh no. It can't be.

No, please no." Kenny lifted his right foot, looked at its bottom and saw the hair.

The hair was curlier and stiffer and blacker than ever. It was coiled on the bottom of his foot, like a wire spring. Kenny leaned against the bed and stood almost upright. He kept his weight on his right foot and took a step with his left foot. So far, so good. He shifted his weight to his left foot and started to take a step with his right foot. BOING! His right leg sprang out from under him. He fell. Kenny grabbed the bed, pulled himself upright and tried again. He fell. *I can't get a sock or shoe on*, he thought. *This can't be covered by a sticker. But it could be covered with a big shoe. If I can get to one.*

He grabbed the bed and pulled himself upright. On his left foot, he hopped to his mom and dad's room. He knocked gently. "Hello," he called softly, "anyone in there?" There was no answer. *Great*, he thought, *they've already gone downstairs.*

He hopped inside the room and took his dad's right tennis shoe from the closet. He hopped back to his room, sat down on the bed and forced his right foot and the hair into the shoe. He tied the shoe very tightly. He found his tennis shoes under his bed and tied the left one on his left foot. He put both feet on the floor. They stayed. He stood up and walked. He walked with a slight limp, but at least he walked.

"Now I can get dressed and go downstairs." He took his pajamas off, pulled a shirt over his head and picked up his jeans from the floor. They wouldn't go on over his mismatched shoes. "What a hassle," he muttered.

He sat on the bed, took the shoes off, lay back on the bed and pulled the jeans up. He knew Valerie zipped her tightest jeans while lying across her bed. Kenny copied her pant-zipping method. Then he sat on the edge of the bed, put the shoes on again and tied the right one in a double knot. He limped downstairs and into the kitchen.

"Mom, Dad, look! Kenny has on one of Dad's tennis shoes!" Valerie was still laughing when she left for school.

Beth Wild looked at her husband. "Jim, I'm so glad you haven't left for work yet. You handle this. I can't stand it. Go on, I'll enjoy watching." Kenny's dad looked at him and waited.

"Last month on 'Hat Day' I had to wear a hat that showed what I wanted to be when I grew up. The month before that on 'Book Day' I had to dress as my favorite book character. Well, see, Dad," Kenny explained, "this is kind of like those times. Only this time it's 'Shoe Day.' I've gotta wear the shoe of the person I most admire and want to be like when I grow up. Everybody at school has to do it today."

He smiled broadly at his father. Mr. Wild smiled proudly back at Kenny and patted him on the shoulder. "That's my boy," he said. "See, Beth, a perfectly reasonable explanation." Kenny's mom rolled her eyes upward and sighed. "Be sure to put my shoe back where it belongs, Kenny."

Kenny left for school, limping. At school, some people made fun of him, but he pretended not to care. Only Pete knew the real reason for Kenny's unusual footwear. At last the day was over. On his way out the classroom door, Kenny saw a wadded-up piece of paper on the floor, next to the trash can. He picked it up, smoothed it out and read:

Dear Krista,
I put an X by the boys I want to go with, you put a check.

☐☐ Donald Sims   ☒☑ Pete Williams
☐☐ Nicholas Webster   ☐☐ Willie Gunder
☐☐ Kenny Wild (over) ☐☐ Matthew Potts
☒☐ Jason Combs   ☐☑ Chuck King
☐☐ Mark Decker   ☒☐ Neil Martin

Your friend - Cindy

Kenny looked for his name. Krista hadn't checked it. She had written "over" next to his name. He turned the paper over. On the back he saw:

His wild hair is really UGLY!

Your friend-
Krista

Kenny tore the paper into a million little pieces before throwing it in the trash. His whole body, even his bones, ached as he trudged slowly home. Once home, he phoned Pete. "I've changed my mind, Pete. I'm going to try the cure. Rubbing a dead cat on my foot couldn't be so bad."

"You have a dead cat right now?"

"No," Kenny answered in a tiny voice.

"What makes you think the hair will still be on your foot when you get a dead cat? With your luck you'll get to rub your nose with it."

"It doesn't matter. I've got to do it. Will you help me find a dead cat?"

"Sure, but how?"

"Tomorrow we'll walk to school on different streets—as many different streets as we can. If we don't find one on the way to school, we'll walk home different ways, too. Okay?"

"Okay."

"And, Pete, don't forget to take a garbage bag or something to carry it in, in case you're the lucky one."

Chapter
Seventeen / Dead-
Cat Search

"You'd think a person could find one dead cat in this town. Is one little dead cat too much to ask for?" Kenny looked disgusted as he threw himself on his bed. Kenny and Pete were exhausted after their dead-cat search, and grounded or not, Kenny was letting Pete rest in his room.

"I know," Pete groaned. "We've looked in every ditch in this town. There are no dead cats anywhere. At least no whole dead cats that a person would want to touch."

"Doesn't Sammy have a stuffed cat?"

"Yeah, Big Bird. But I don't think a stuffed cat would work. Besides, Sammy can't fall asleep without Big Bird. And I always say, the more Sammy sleeps, the better."

Valerie opened the door to Kenny's room, stuck her head inside and said, "Hey, twerp. Have you seen my green sweatshirt? I thought you, its former owner, might have it."

"I can't hear you. You didn't knock first."

"Thanks. You've been a big help, as usual," Valerie snarled. She slammed the door as she left.

"Pete," Kenny said, "I just figured out where we can get a dead cat."

"Great! Where?"

"From Val."

"Oh, sure. I guess she keeps one in her room. In case she gets hungry."

"I'm serious. She's dissecting one in biology class."

"Will she let you have it?"

Kenny took his ruined green sweatshirt from under his mattress, where he'd hidden it. "Let's find out," he said.

They marched across the hall to Valerie's room. Kenny knocked gently on her door. "Oh, Val," he said sweetly. "I found your sweatshirt."

She opened the door and stood in the doorway, so they couldn't come inside.

"Great." She grabbed the sweatshirt out of his hands. "What happened? Did you suddenly remember where you hid it?"

Kenny got right to the point. "Can I have your dead cat when you finish dissecting it?"

So did Valerie. "What's it worth to you?"

"Anything!" Pete exclaimed. "He'll do anyth . . ."

"Not much, really." Kenny interrupted. "I thought I might take it to school. You know science is Mrs. Welty's favorite subject. But don't tell Mom and Dad I want it."

"Hmm, 'not much,' and 'anything.' That's interesting. I'll think about it." She slammed the door in their faces.

"Thanks, Pete. Now she knows how much I really want it."

"Sounds like she won't let you have it."

"Oh, she'll let me have it, all right. But it's going to cost me. Big."

Chapter Eighteen / The Cure

Kenny went to bed without a dead cat. Valerie was still thinking about giving him her biology leftovers. The next morning, Kenny didn't want to get out of bed without knowing if the hair had moved. He touched his right foot and felt the hair. *Rats,* he thought, *it's still there! Wait, it could be worse. If I do get a dead cat, I'd much rather rub it on my foot than anywhere else.*

Once again, Kenny had to wear his dad's right tennis shoe in order to walk downstairs to breakfast, or to walk anywhere.

"Good morning, Kenny," his mom said. "Care to join us?"

"You bet." Kenny got a bowl of Wheaties and sat down quickly. He wanted his feet hidden under the table before Valerie noticed his mismatched shoes.

"Is it Shoe Day again, Kenny?" Valerie asked sarcastically.

She notices everything, Kenny thought. Out loud he said, "Yeah, as a matter of fact, it is. Yesterday's shoe day was so much fun we're doing it again today." He showed Valerie he too could be sarcastic by adding, "Thanks for asking."

What she said next was worse than sarcasm. "I've been thinking about you know what, Kenny, and I've decided what I'm going to do."

"Fine."

"Don't you want to know what I've decided?"

"No. Tell me later," he said pleadingly, "when we're alone."

"What is the 'you know what' you've been thinking about?" Mr. Wild asked.

"It's private, Dad." Valerie explained.

"Okay. I guess you kids are entitled to your privacy, same as your mom and me."

Kenny finished eating, said good-bye and limped off to school. "Well?" Pete asked, the minute he saw Kenny. "Did Val decide to let you have her biology garbage?"

"I don't know. She started talking about it in front of Mom and Dad. I could have killed her. If Valerie tells them what I told her about why I want the cat, they'll think it's neat. I'll really have to bring a dead cat—a dead pickled, dissected cat—to school!" The tardy bell rang. Kenny risked one last whisper. "I'll call you as soon as I find out anything new."

"No talking after the tardy bell rings. I'm gonna tell," Donald hissed. He waved his hand frantically at their teacher, "Mrs. Welty! Mrs. Welty! Kenny was talking after the tardy bell rang."

"Donald, come put your name on the board. You lose recess time for talking without permission after the tardy bell rang." Mrs. Welty said.

When the dismissal bell rang, Kenny rushed home and waited for Valerie to arrive. Finally, the door to his room opened and an arm holding a plastic garbage bag was shoved through the opening.

"Here it is, twerp," Valerie's voice said. The rest of her appeared in the doorway. She stood there and swung the bag back and forth. "I told my teacher my nerdy little brother wanted my cat to show his grade school teacher. She thought that was so wonderful she insisted I bring you an unused cat. You're lucky, it doesn't even stink. It's still sealed inside the plastic bag."

"Not so loud and get in here." Kenny reached for the bag. "I don't want Mom and Dad to hear."

Valerie came into Kenny's room. "Well, you're welcome, I'm sure." She snatched the

bag away. "Not so fast. I'm not giving it to you, I'm trading it to you."

"Trading it for what?" Kenny asked. He was afraid he already knew the answer.

"Guess."

"For my Skulls ticket?"

"For your Skulls ticket."

"You won't take anything else, like money?"

"No."

"I'll get the ticket, but you have to turn around. It's in my secret hiding place." Valerie turned. Kenny made a lot of noise rummaging through a drawer while he quietly took the ticket from behind the Skulls poster hanging above his desk. "You can look now. Here, take it."

Valerie handed Kenny the cat. "Here's your cat. I hope it's worth it."

As soon as Valerie left, Kenny phoned Pete. "Pete, I got it. She made me trade my Skulls ticket for it. Can you sneak out and meet me at midnight? We have to bury the cat in moonlight."

"Sure. I'll meet you in your backyard at midnight. Let's synchronize our watches. I don't want you waiting alone in the dark." Pete had been reading the monster book he checked out in library class.

"And, Pete, read the cure's saying to me. I want to memorize it."

Kenny set his alarm for 11:45 P.M. and tried to sleep. He only tossed and turned. Finally, it was midnight. Kenny snuck out of his house with the cat and a shovel.

"Kenny, I'm here, over here," Pete whispered. He stood under the tree closest to the Wilds' back door. They walked to the far edge of Kenny's yard.

"Let's get this over with, quick," Kenny said as he opened the garbage bag.

"Where's a flashlight? I can't believe you didn't bring a flashlight. How can we see the cat?"

"Believe it. I don't want to see the cat. I've figured out a way to do this so I won't have to see the cat." Kenny sat on the lawn and took his dad's shoe off his right foot. "You hold the garbage bag open, I'll stick my foot in and rub it against the cat."

"Are you sure that's okay? The cure said to rub the cat against the hair, not the hair against the cat. Besides, the cat's floating around in a plastic bag full of formaldehyde."

"No, I'm not sure. But it'll have to do."

While Pete held the garbage bag open, Kenny stuck his bare foot inside, rubbed the hair against the plastic-covered cat and shivered. As he shivered and rubbed, he said very, very fast, faster than he'd ever said anything in his whole life, "Hair, hair go away. Don't come again any day."

"Do you think once is enough?"

"Once is more than enough." Kenny put his dad's shoe back on and stood up. "Help me dig a hole, but be quiet." They worked quietly and quickly and soon had the cat buried. "Thanks, Pete. I'll see ya at school."

"Sure, Kenny. Good night."

Back in his room, Kenny studied his image in the mirror on his door and thought about Dr. Shoemaker. *Dr. Shoemaker said I'd have the wild hair until I found something more important to me than having slightly messy hair.* Krista's face popped into his mind and he thought about her as he stared in the mirror. *Maybe she's right,* he thought, *maybe my hair is ugly.* Kenny combed his wild hair until it lay neat and flat on his head *That wasn't so bad,* he thought, *I might do it again.*

Chapter
Nineteen / Hair Today,
Gone Tomorrow

Kenny fell asleep in an instant and slept deeply until he heard pounding on his door and his mother calling, "Get up, Kenny. You've overslept. Hurry or you'll be late for school." Kenny jumped out of bed, got dressed, combed his hair and rushed downstairs.

"Good morning, Kenny," his dad greeted him cheerfully.

"Good morning, everybody," Kenny said.

"No Shoe Day, no walking sticker album today?" Valerie asked. "Ah, but aren't we missing something?"

"The hair!" Kenny exclaimed. "It's gone!"

"Hair? What hair?" Mr. Wild asked.

"Did I say hair?" Kenny asked. "I meant to say 'there.' Look there. He pointed out the window. Everyone looked.

"What? Oh, I see now. Look at that, Jim. Someone's been digging in the backyard," Kenny's mom said.

Oh, no, good going, stupid, why couldn't you have pointed at the ceiling or the floor, anywhere but the backyard, Kenny scolded himself.

"I'd better go check it out." Mr. Wild started to get up.

"I meant the cat," Valerie interrupted. "Where's the cat for Mrs. Welty?"

"Don't bother, Dad. It was me. I dug in the backyard last night. I'm sorry, I had to sneak out of the house to do it because I'm grounded."

"You're sorry? You're sorry you HAD to sneak around or you're sorry you snuck around?" Mrs. Wild asked.

"Both."

"And what, may I ask were you burying?"

"The cat."

"What cat." Kenny's parents asked at the same time.

"My cat! Of all the nerve!" Valerie exclaimed

"It's not your cat. I paid for it, so I can do anything I want with it. I felt sorry for it, Val. I thought it was better to bury it than give it to Mrs. Welty, even though she would have liked it. I gave it a decent burial, so sue me."

"Stop! I want an explanation and I want it now. And it better be good," Mr. Wild warned. He crossed his arms, leaned back in his chair and glared at Kenny.

Chapter
Twenty / Love, or a
Dead Cat?

Kenny told his parents about his wish on Dr. Shoemaker's magic stone. He told them about the strange results from the wish and about the dead-cat cure and how he got the cat. In short, he told them everything, even about combing his hair.

"What an imagination!" Mrs. Wild exclaimed.

"Really, Kenny, you don't expect us to believe any of that, do you?" Mr. Wild asked. "It's okay if you want to give Mrs. Welty a present, then change your mind and not give it to her, although a dead cat is an unusual gift."

"You don't need to be embarrassed about it and make up a big story," Mrs. Wild added. "And we're delighted you combed your hair. I can't believe we didn't notice. I think any child who trades a Skulls ticket for a gift for his teacher deserves a reward."

"I agree," Mr. Wild said. "We can't get you another ticket, but we can suspend your grounding." He stood and waved his arms in the air. "I now declare you officially ungrounded."

Kenny was stunned. They didn't believe him. They didn't believe any of his explanation. He decided not to argue. "Great! You're the best parents in the world. Thanks! I gotta go. Thanks again." If his parents thought he was telling a big story, so be it. *Why look a gift horse in the mouth*, he thought. Kenny ran all the way to Westdale and sat down just as the tardy bell rang. Pete looked over at Kenny's feet, then at his friend's smiling face.

"It worked! It worked! Didn't it?" he whispered excitedly.

Kenny whispered back, "Something worked. The hair is gone." Kenny noticed Donald Sims glaring at them.

"All right, Pete and Kenny, you lose recess time. Put your names on the board." Mrs. Welty caught them breaking her most unbreakable rule—no talking after the tardy bell rang. Kenny was so happy he didn't mind. He smiled all the way to the board and back. As he sat down, he noticed Krista staring at him. She smiled at him before looking away. His smile grew bigger.

At recess, Pete and Kenny stood against

one wall of the school building, serving their time. Kenny stood one legged, leaning against the wall, and told Pete about his morning at home. "The funny thing is, not one person in my family noticed that I'd combed my hair. Mom and Dad promised not to mention hair again, but Valerie didn't and she notices everything."

"She just notices everything that could get you in trouble," Pete said. "I didn't notice. It's funny—I mean funny weird, not funny ha ha—but if you're real close to a person and see them every day, you don't notice things that are different about them. Not right away, anyway."

"Yeah, I remember when Mom stopped smoking. It was two weeks before Dad or I noticed. Of course Val claimed she noticed right away."

"And when my dad shaved off his beard. None of my family said anything. He had to make us notice." Pete frowned and asked, "Why did you comb your hair?"

"I found something more important to me than not combing my hair."

"What?"

"That's personal," Kenny said and smiled.

"Hey, slimer's looking at us." Pete nodded toward Krista, who stood over by the swings, next to Cindy. "No, she's looking at you and she's smiling!"

"Don't call her that. She's not stuck up. She's just shy."

"All right," Mrs. Welty called. "You two have served your time. You're free." She shook her head and spoke to the other playground-duty teacher, "Free, that is, until tomorrow's recess. Those two seem to never learn."

Kenny and Pete ran to join their friends in a soccer game. Before they could score any points for their team, Mrs. Welty blew her whistle. Recess was over. The class lined up and walked slowly into their room. Kenny and Pete were the last two in line.

When Kenny sat down, he noticed a folded note lying on top of his desk. Kenny opened the note, read it and smiled. His heart began to thump loudly. The note said, "Krista likes you. She wants you to meet her at the skating rink tonight. Will you?" It was signed "Cindy."

Kenny folded the note carefully and put it in his pocket. This note he would keep forever. He turned around in his seat. "Psst, Cindy," he whispered, "tell her yes. The answer is yes." He was sure his parents would let him go. After all, he was officially ungrounded.

He turned and looked over at Krista. She was looking at him. They smiled at each other until Mrs. Welty's voice pulled their eyes to the front of the room. "Donald, please don't ask me if you can do anything else today!" Donald Sims stood in his favorite place, in front of Mrs. Welty's desk. Mrs. Welty noticed the rest of her class watching, and lowered her voice. "I've let you feed the tarantula, empty the trash can and, oh, I can't remember, there's so many things you've 'helped' me with. Just sit down. The only help I need right now is for you to sit down and not ask to do anything else."

Hmm, Donald Sims, Kenny thought, *why not? He would make a good Helpfulness Plot. Yeah, Mrs. Welty needs help keeping Donald out of her hair. I only promised Dad I wouldn't use HPs on him and Mom and Val. I never said anything about Mrs. Welty. An HP for Mrs. Welty is just what I need to keep me off the wall at recess.* Happily, Kenny leaned back and began planning his Donald Sims HP. *Maybe Dr. Shoemaker could help me with Donald,* Kenny thought. *I might go see her after school. We could talk about Donald and I could tell her about my wild hair.*

"I need two volunteers to hang our solar system posters on the walls outside the classroom," Mrs. Welty said. A field of waving hands appeared above her students' heads.

"Sit down, Donald. Don't even think about it. Kenny, you and Krista may hang the posters." Kenny's heart raced as he and Krista walked into the hall. They carried the posters, a tape dispenser, and a chair with them.

"Here"—Krista handed the posters and tape dispenser to Kenny—"you put tape on the posters and I'll hang them. My mom says I have an 'artistic eye' for that sort of thing." Krista climbed on the chair and waited for Kenny to hand her a poster.

"Which one is it?" Kenny asked. He pulled some tape off, rolled it and stuck it on the back of a poster. He handed the taped poster to Krista.

"Which one is what?" Krista asked as she hung the poster.

"Which eye, right or left?" Kenny looked up at Krista and grinned.

"Oh, I get it. That's funny." Krista laughed. "You're funny. You sure do some strange things, but you're nice. You never call me slimer or stuck up or anything bad. I like you. Your hair looks good today. You combed it, didn't you?" She glanced over Kenny's head. "Look"—Kenny turned and saw a person walking toward them—"there's Dr. Shoemaker."

"You know her?"

"Sure, I talk to her sometimes when I'm upset about being called slimer or something. She's nice. Hi, Dr. Shoemaker."

"Hello, Krista. Hello, Kenny." Dr. Shoemaker noticed Kenny's neatly combed hair and his happy face. "Well, Kenny, I see you've changed. Someday you should stop by my office and tell me what you found that's more important to you than your 'slightly messy' hair." She looked at Krista's smiling face. "Hmm, I think I know. Good-bye, you two. Do come visit me sometime." She walked on down the hall.

"I will, Dr. Shoemaker," Kenny called after her. "I have something important to discuss with you. Something to help Mrs. Welty," he spoke louder as Dr. Shoemaker got further and further away. "Actually, it's an HP, a Helpfulness Plot. I'll tell you all about it, soon."

About the Author

A native of the Ozark Mountain region of Arkansas, Janet Greeson is married and currently working as a School Media Specialist at the Westwood Elementary School in Springdale, Arizona, a position she has held for the past nine years.

Ms. Greeson attended the University of Arkansas, where she received her B.A. in Art, and then an Ed.S. in Instructional Resources. Travel is her favorite pastime, and in addition to extensive travel in the United States, Canada, and Mexico, she has explored regions of India, Guatemala, and England.

Kenny Wild's Hair is her first work of children's fiction.

F
GRE

Greeson, Janet.

Kenny Wild's hair

DATE DUE	BORROWER'S NAME	ROOM NUMBER
APR 3 1996	Christina H.	6-320

F
GRE

Greeson, Janet.

Kenny Wild's hair